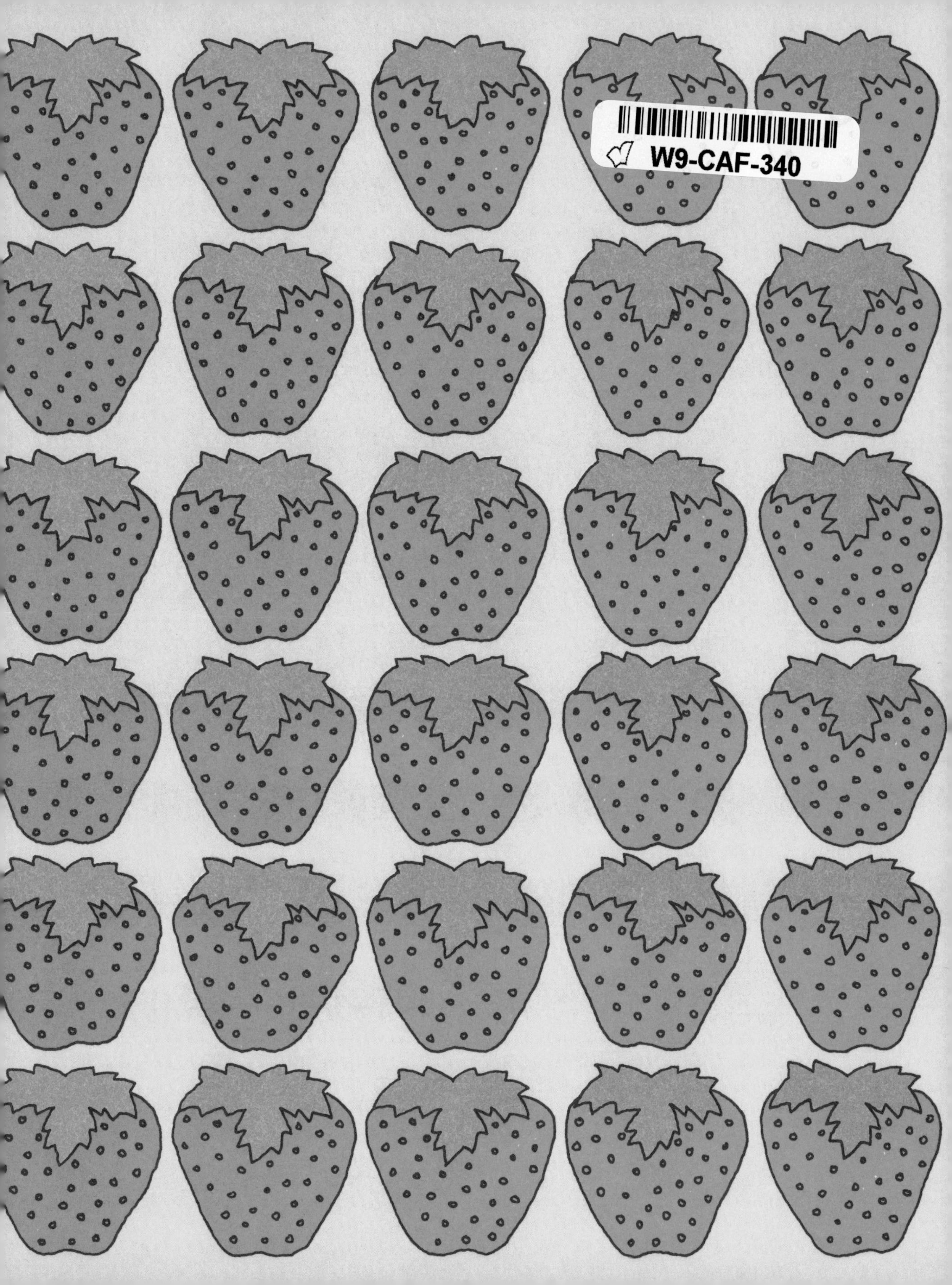
W9-CAF-340

THE STICKYBEAR FAMILY™
Bedford Stickybear
Sara Stickybear
Bumper Stickybear

this
strawberry library
of first learning
book
belongs to
Kristen
COOK

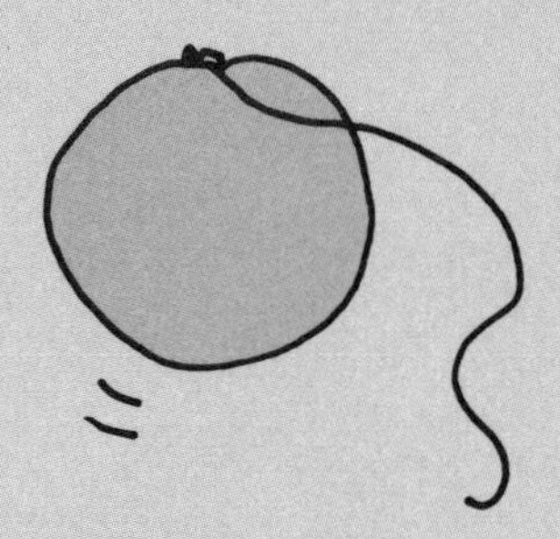

Copyright © 1983 by Optimum Resource, Inc.,
Norfolk, Connecticut
All rights reserved.
No part of this publication may be reproduced,
stored in a retrieval system, or transmitted
in any form or by any means, electronic, mechanical,
photocopying, recording, or otherwise, without the
prior written permission of the publisher.

Printed in the United States of America.

Stickybear™ is the registered trademark of Optimum Resource, Inc.
Strawberry® and A Strawberry Book® are the registered
trademarks of One Strawberry, Inc.

Weekly Reader Books' Edition

Library of Congress Cataloging in Publication Data

Hefter, Richard.
Bears away from home.

(Stickybear books)
Summary: the Stickybear family travels on
vacation to places that the children love.
[1. Vacations—Fiction. 2. Bears—Fiction]
I. Title. II. Series: Hefter, Richard. Stickybear
books.
PZ7.H3587Be 1983 [E] 83-4149
ISBN 0-911787-05-4

bears away from home

by Richard Hefter

Optimum Resource, Inc. • Connecticut

The Stickybear family is going on a vacation.
Cousin Tizzy is going too.
She is trying to pack her goldfish.

The bears are on the road.
Tizzy is hungry.

FOOD
FUEL
5
MILES

The Stickybears stop for some fast food.
Tizzy and Bumper like the french fries best.

PICK-UP HERE
DRIVE
THRU

The children are spending their
first night in a motel.
Bumper is excited.
Tizzy is messy.

Breakfast tastes really good when you eat it outside.

Eggs

Tizzy and Bumper are going swimming.
They love the beach.

The beach is the best place in the world to build sand castles!

It’s morning again, and the
Stickybears are going to the fair.
Look at the horses.
Look at the cows.

COUNTY FAIR
1 MI.

Bumper wants to go on the rides.
Tizzy wants to buy a hat and a flag.

FAIR
RIDES
LIVESTOC
HATS
T-SHIR
FLA
COUNTY
FAIR
COUN
FAIR

The bears are
high up in the air!

FAIR

Back at the motel, it's time for a nice swim in the pool.

5

The Stickybears are spending today at a wonderful western town.

This will be a funny photograph!

WESTERN TOWN
SOUVENIRS
SALOON
TRAIN RIDES
PIRATES COVE

VIDEO
CITY

Bumper and Tizzy love video arcades. Stickybear thinks they are noisy.

It’s time to go home.

COUNTY FAIR
VIDEO

Home
Sweet
Home

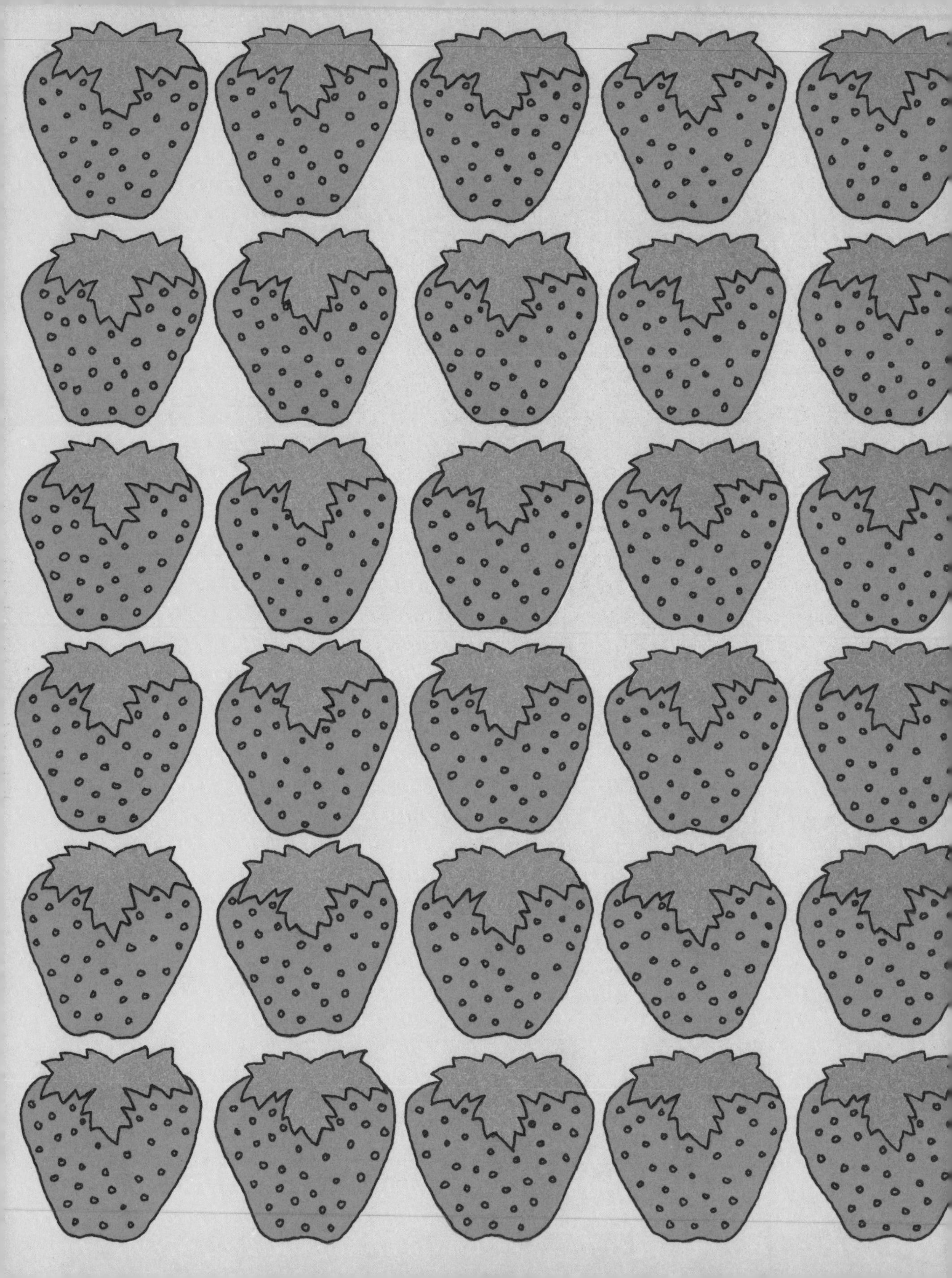